325 Alex:
Cougar Sightings

© 2024 Shawn L. Bird
ISBN 978-1-989642-43-6 paperback
ISBN 978-1-989642-48-1 ebook

Lintusen Press
lintusenpress@shaw.ca
PO Box 10019 Salmon Arm, BC V1E 3B9

Originally published as a serial in the *Salmon Arm Friday A.M.* newspaper March 15 to December 20, 2024

SHAWN L. BIRD

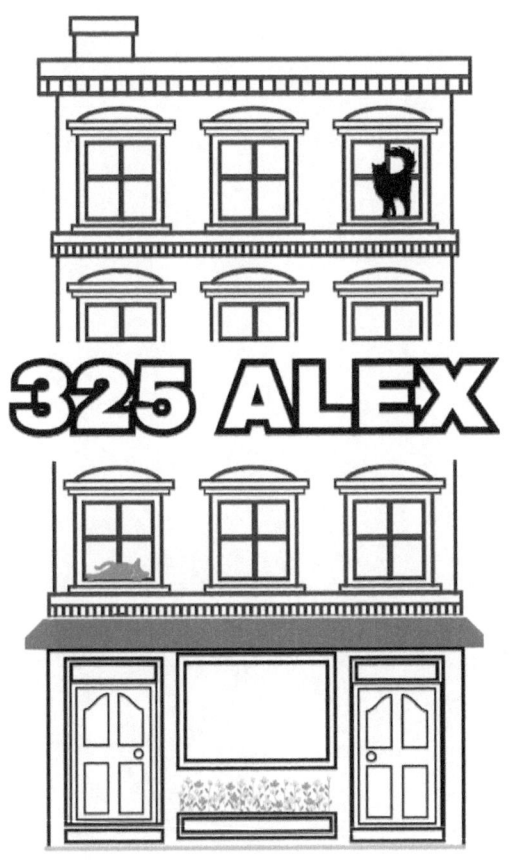

325 ALEX

Cougar Sightings

RESIDENTS OF 325 ALEX STREET

#100
vacant store front

#201
The college students:
Chris
Mabel
Dimity
Marcus

#202
Shirley John
her small, stealthy, tawny cat "Cougar"

#301
Henry Block

#302
dela Cruz family:
Angelo
Sofia
Margarita (Maggie)

#401
Susanne Winters
the neighbourhood sentinel, tuxedo cat, "Artemis"

#402
The Empty Apartment

THE GROUND FLOOR LAYOUT:

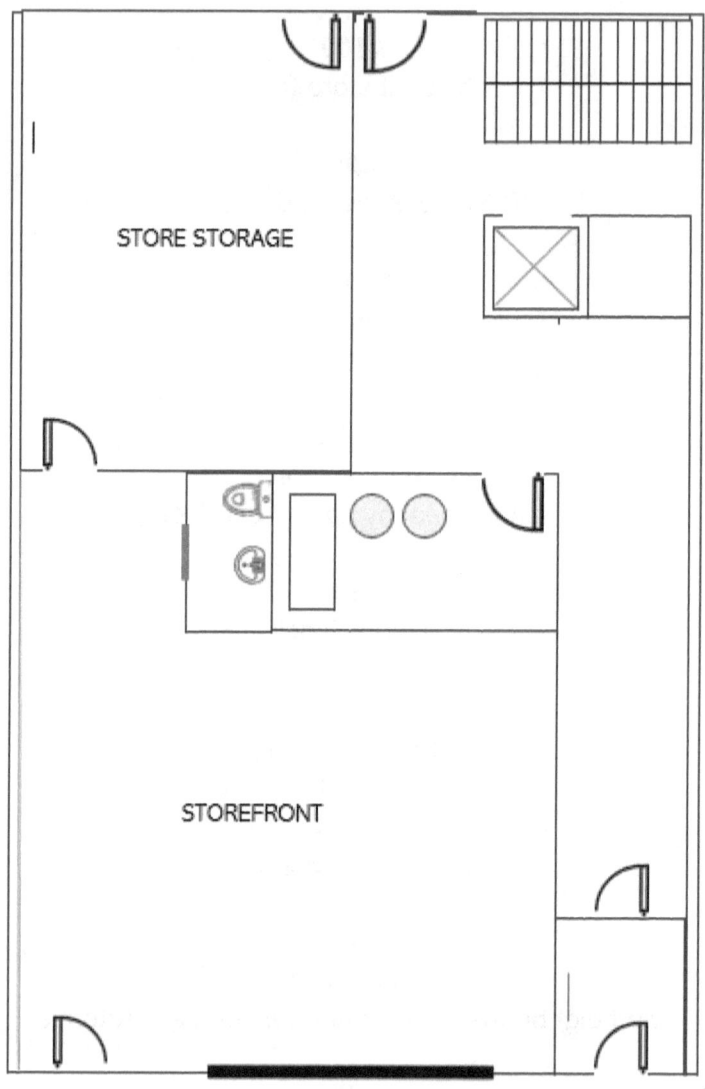

THE APARTMENT FLOORS LAYOUT:

 # -02   **# -01**

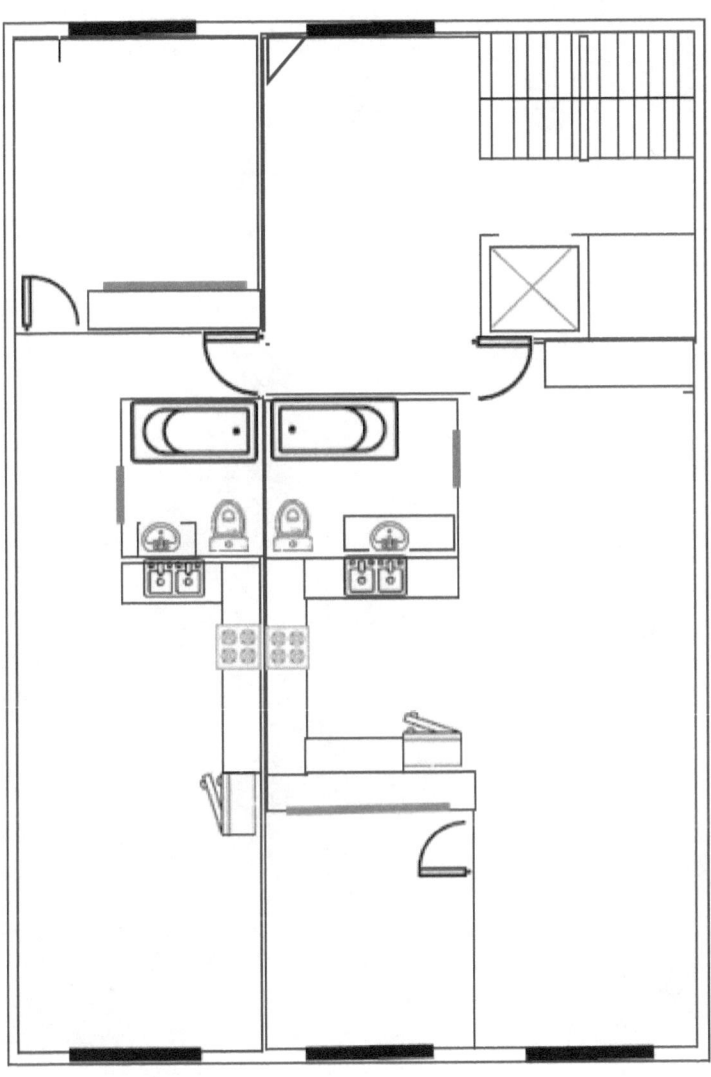

BIG NEWS
#1

Originally scheduled: March 15, 2024

Artemis gazed from her cat tree in suite #401 of 325 Alex Street. From here, she could see all.

Lorne was walking with a stack of his weekly newspaper, his wheaton-poodle cross Lexi following at his heels. He entered the pie shop.

The apartment door rattled. "Susanne! You won't believe it!"

Artemis ignored it.

Lorne emerged and glanced up. He saw Artemis watching and waved. She appreciated those who knew how to honour the superiority of cats.

Lexi did not look up. Dogs rarely did, unless they were trying to catch a ball.

The apartment door rattled again. Artemis jumped off her perch, hissing.

"Come on, Susanne! Open up! I've got news!"

It was Henry, who lived below them in 301.

He knocked, waited, and then muttered. "Damn. I guess you're not there."

Artemis heard steps in the hall, and then, "Oh! There you are!"

"Hi, Henry. Let me get my groceries in."

Susanne pushed open the door, puffing from the

stairs. "The landlord needs to fix that elevator," she said.

Artemis began to weave between her legs, covering Susanne with the scent of belonging.

Susanne stumbled into the kitchen. She set her cloth Askews bags on the counter and leaned down to pick up the cat. "Silly girl," she murmured into her fur. "What did you want Henry?"

"They've rented #402!"

Susanne blinked. "They can't rent #402. It's unethical."

"Apparently they disclosed everything. They're giving them a rent deduction."

"I wouldn't live there for free." She shuddered.

"How long do you think they'll last?"

"A month?" suggested Susanne

"Ten bucks says not even two weeks."

"Deal." They shook.

"Poor sap," said Henry.

Artemis yowled her agreement.

GOT A DATE
#2

Originally scheduled: March 22, 2024

Susanne yawned as she stood in the café line, alternately admiring the pies in the case and contemplating the menu board above the counter. The baby on the third floor had been crying all night.

"The usual?" Nic said, when she was finally at the front. "Quiche and coffee, two cream, one sugar?"

Susanne laughed. "Yeah, perfect."

"I hear you have a new neighbour coming," he said as he punched in the order. "I thought they'd never be able to rent that unit."

"Me, neither," she said, taking the coffee.

She sat at a table, facing the street, sipping. A tall young man with a pencil thin moustache swept the street with earnest focus. She saw Henry, her downstairs neighbour, and pulled into the corner, hoping he wouldn't look this way.

The marquee across the road announced the film society showings. She checked her phone to read about the options, thinking she could use a distraction.

Nic set the quiche on the table. "Listen, I wonder if you'd like to see a movie?" He gave a nod to the marquee. Tonight's looks good."

Susanne nodded, "I was thinking I'd like to see it. Yes."

As she ate her quiche, a text came in: Henry inviting her to the same movie.

"Sorry. Got a date," she typed back.

She shut off the phone and put it in her pocket. She didn't want to know Henry's reaction. She stood up.

Nic looked up from washing a table. "I"ll meet you out front at 6:30!" .

She nodded and stepped onto Alex Street, wondering how long she could hide before she had to deal with this trouble.

ENTERTAINING?
#3

Originally scheduled: April 3, 2024

Henry Block woke groaning to his alarm blaring the *Star Wars* theme. He'd had two hours of sleep. Little Maggie next door was teething and she was not happy about it. Consequently, no one else at 325 Alex Street was happy about it either. Were that not bad enough, before Maggie's howls had pierced the night, he'd been tossing and turning over Susanne.

He wasn't ashamed to admit he'd spied on her. He'd turned the lights out in his apartment and sat staring out his window to see who picked her up for that date. He was delighted when, at 6:25, she walked out of the building alone. Unfortunately, at 6:29 he saw her in front of the Salmar embracing Nic from the pie place. It was just a friendly hug, Henry'd decided, but when the movie let out, they'd emerged holding hands and five minutes later Henry had heard their laughter on the stairs.

As he poured hot water into his French press, there was a thump on his ceiling, likely Artemis the cat knocking things over. He ate breakfast wondering when Susanne's new neighbour would be moving in, and pondered whether they were brave or just stupid to rent that suite.

When he left for work, a jovial voice called from the stairwell, "Hello, Henry!"

Henry scowled at Nic. He didn't want to think about why he was still in their building nor why he was in such a good mood.

Nic grinned as they descended together, "You!"

"Excuse me?"

Nic waved down the hall to the second floor suites. "Susanne was telling me last night about how entertaining she finds you! I had no idea. "

Henry froze on the step as Nic pushed cheerily out onto Alex Street.

He wanted Susanne to find him attractive, considerate, fascinating.

Entertaining.

That didn't sound good at all.

IT'S NOT VANCOUVER #4

Originally scheduled: April 12, 2024

When Chris had told Marcus they had room for him to stay while he did his welding course at Okanagan College, he'd thought they'd meant an extra bedroom. When Chris had pointed to the couch, Marcus presumed it was a hide-a-bed, but no. He was to sleep on Chris's six foot long couch, which might have been fine if Marcus were five feet tall, but Marcus was six foot three.

Mabel and Dimity were tiny, but they had beds. There were three beds in the tiny bedroom. He tried not to be jealous. Beggers didn't choose, after all.

Chris had assured him there was a bus that would take him from downtown to the college.

Imagine his surprise when the route labeled 'Okanagan College' only went to the academic campus, not to the trades campus in the industrial park. The closest transit could get him was thirty-three blocks away. A good hour's walk. Thankfully, he'd found a folding bike at Churches' Thrift Store, so when the roads were clear, he could cycle the final five kilometres. In February, he'd had a long, cold, and snowy walk. But now it was April and he was thankful for the rickety bike.

At least it wasn't Vancouver.

As he tried to get comfortable enough to sleep, he told

himself he was lucky to have a place to stay. Still. There was something strange going on in this building. The screaming baby in the suite above gave him the creeps, and he kept hearing murmurs about suite #402.

The landlord had heard he was a welding student and emailed to ask if he were handy, because there were some repairs to be done before the new tenant arrived. Marcus said he'd look.

Maybe he'd solve his money problems and the mystery of #402.

THINGS HAPPENED
#5

Originally scheduled: April 19, 2024

Shirley John had lived all her life in Salmon Arm. She'd had some adventures, like as a student at the old SASS when she'd snuck in three pigs numbered 1, 2, and 4 or the time she hitchhiked to Vancouver and accidentally stole a car, but mostly she'd kept her head down and stayed out of trouble.

She kept a careful watch on things at 325 Alex. The street level store-front had been empty for nearly a year since the marijuana store closed. Shirley didn't miss the skunky stink wafting up the back stairs, though she'd appreciated the senior's discount on the CBD oil. Somedays, passing the store-front she felt a little guilty. Those boys might have stuck around if she hadn't inadvertently tasered one of them after hours, but sometimes things just happened.

Like when the old gal she'd worked for had lost her jewelry box and had the whole staff fingerprinted at the old RCMP station, and in return for the indignity, Shirley had anonymously reported her to the city for illegally sleeping in her business premises. Things happen.

It amused Shirley to keep a low profile in the building. She didn't think any of the other tenants had ever seen her, but she made sure to know them all. Things happened.

Soon there'd be a new tenant for the empty suite on the fourth floor. It was about time things moved along. She hoped it'd be okay.

Shirley patted her little tawny cat. The summer she'd gotten a kitten there'd been a cougar roaming the town, so she'd called the kitten 'Cougar,' and thought it was very clever.

She grabbed her Askew's bag, and once she was sure no one was in the halls or stairs, slipped out. On the street, she studied the store-front. Perhaps she could start a business herself? She was bored with retirement. Maybe she could be a private investigator or a consultant? She gave good advice, whenever anyone bothered to ask, at least.

Up ahead on Lakeshore, she saw the nice young man from the third floor. He was certainly headed for a fall with the way he mooned over the girl on the fourth floor. She hoped he'd be okay. But though it was unfortunate, things happened.

TIME FOR AN EXORCIST?
#6

Originally scheduled: May 3, 2024

Tiny Margarita Maria Mai dela Cruz was trying to tell her parents.

Would they listen?

They would not.

The more she shrieked fit to bring the house down, trying to convey to them their peril, the more they insisted on rubbing concoctions on her gums, rocking her with shushes while they murmured, 'It'll be okay Maggie Mai.'

Maggie knew that it would absolutely not be okay.

Above their heads danger was growing.

Could they not feel it?

There was a cat on the floor above and one on the floor below. Maggie felt sure that the cats understood. Sometimes she heard their sympathetic yowls.

But the humans? Not one of the adult humans in the building appreciated the urgency.

They were all in trouble.

In the darkness, Maggie pinched her eyes tight closed and wailed.

Angelo delaCruz walked back and forth in the small apartment trying to comfort his daughter, while his wife attempted to sleep in their only bedroom. He'd never heard of a child who screamed so loudly and so constantly. Sweet Maggie was loved, cuddled, changed, fed, and cuddled some more. But still she whimpered or screeched. The doctors tested for allergies, injuries, and everything else they could think of. Finally they announced it was "just colic." Just. As if something causing so much misery was 'just' anything.

Perhaps fresh air would help. He wrapped Maggie up and stepped into the hall. A blurry movement from the stairwell made him jump. "Hello? Is someone there?" No one answered. Warily, he headed outside. A walk around McGuire Lake would be just the thing. They weren't five steps from the building when Maggie heaved a great sigh and stopped crying.

He wondered if perhaps there was something wrong with the apartment. Maybe he should see if there was an exorcist available. The Church still had exorcists, didn't it?

BOXES
#7

Originally scheduled: May 10, 2024

In the early morning dim on his way to welding class, Marcus tripped over the box beside the front door, but caught himself before he fell. His thrift store folding bike landed hard but he checked it carefully and it didn't seem too bent to function. He pushed the box down the wall to the dead elevator and headed to the bus stop on Lakeshore.

Shirley John tripped over the box at the bottom of the stairs at nine o'clock. She grabbed the railing before calamity. She examined the label and shuddered. She didn't want anything to do with that. She nudged it out of the way and headed off to Hudson Street pick up her prescriptions.

Sofia dela Cruz stumbled against the box on the second floor landing at ten o'clock. With a whimpering Maggie strapped to her back, she muttered about inconsiderate tenants and kicked it in front of 201 where the students lived. Maggie began to cry. Sofia headed down the stairs, hoping that a walk on the SABNES trail would lull the baby to sleep.

Chris, Mabel, and Dimity noticed the box that blocked their door at noon, but they just jumped over it. Their sessions at Okanagan College were finished until

September and they were off to the student employment office to see if there were any fun, well-paying summer jobs on offer. Dimity wanted to check out the music store and see about advanced guitar lessons. She had an itch to start a band.

Mid-afternoon, Henry left his third floor apartment and was scrolling through his phone looking wishfully for a text from Susanne, when he tripped over the box and went sprawling down two flights of stairs.

WARNINGS
#8

Originally scheduled: May 17, 2024

Chris was standing outside 325 Alex Street staring after the departing ambulance when Susanne come through the passage from the Ross Street parkade. "Susanne!" they called across the road. "It's awful!"

"Oh?" she said joining him on the sidewalk. "What's awful?"

"It's Henry. Mabel called the ambulance when she found him sprawled on the second floor landing."

Susanne gasped. "What happened?"

"We think he fell down the stairs."

They both looked up the stairwell and shivered.

"That's horrible. Was he okay?"

Chris shook their head. "He was unconscious. The paramedics just took him away."

"I wonder what happened?" Susanne asked as they walked up the stairs, each holding firmly to the banister.

Chris walked to their apartment on the second floor and shrugged. "No idea. Hope it isn't a ghost or something!"

They laughed awkwardly as Chris shut their door and Susanne kept going up to the top floor.

When she arrived at #401 there was a box in front of her door. "Cool!" she thought, "someone remembered my birthday!" She brought it into her suite.

Artemis stood on her cat tree staring at the box with her back arched and hackles raised.

"What's wrong with you, cat?" Susanne said.

Artemis jumped down and stalked cautiously toward the box, whiskers trembling. She stretched her nose, touched the it, and then leapt back hissing.

"What on earth?" said Susanne. She read the label:

Occupant
#402-325 Alex Street.

"Oh crap." She gasped. "Crap, crap, crap!"

She pushed the box into the hall and in front of #402.

She slammed her door and leaned against it, breathing heavily. "Thank you, Artemis," she said.

But Artemis ignored her. She was back on her cat tree, curled up on the top tier pretending to be asleep.

CHANGES
#9

Originally scheduled: May 24, 2024

From behind the till, Nic was watching the café door for Susanne when Lorne came in to drop off a stack of Friday AM papers. His friend Todd stood outside with Lexi. "Any good news?" Nic asked.

"Sure," Lorne said. "Lots of kindnesses being reported, and they're looking for new acts for Wednesday on the Wharf. Why don't you try out?"

Nic laughed and waved as they went on their way. He thought about performing. He wished he had the confidence even to try performing at a community hall coffee house. Meanwhile, there were Mabel and Dimity practicing their bass and guitar duets like they were going to be the next Salmon Armenians.

Susanne came through the door then and got in line.

"Quiche and coffee?" he asked when it was her turn.

"How's the soup?"

He hid his surprise at the uncharacteric question. "It's almost sold out."

"Soup, then," she said with a decisive nod, "and an iced coffee, please."

"Changing times?" he said as he handed her the keypad.

She just smiled.

"How's the new neighbour?" he asked.

Susanne shrugged. "No idea. I don't think anyone has seen them yet."

Nic busied himself with her drink and then handed it across. "My offer still stands. If you need to get out of there, you're welcome at my place."

"Thanks," she said, but she didn't meet his eyes. "I'll sit on the other side."

He watched her go into the addition with her drink, her shoulders hunched and eyes down. She'd lost her spark, he thought. Why? It wouldn't be because of boxes stacking up at the end of her hall. No one would be worried about a little thing like that, would they? Was there something else?

A MIRACLE
#10

Originally scheduled: June 7, 2024

Henry stood balancing on crutches at the entrance to 325 Alex Street working up the courage to go inside. He wished he didn't live on the third floor. But there was no help for it. He'd fallen down the stairs, whacked his head hard enough that he'd been out cold for an hour, and damaged something important in his left knee.

Crutches were horrible, painful things that made the simplest exursion exhausting, but they were what he had. He pondered the merits of scooching up step by step on his backside versus holding two crutches in one arm while he gripped the handrail versus using two crutches but no handrail.

Mabel joined him on the sidewalk. She had an instrument case slung on her back. "Oooh. Crutches. That sucks."

"It does," Henry agreed. "But stairs suck more."

"Then I have good news for you. The elevator works."

"Oh, thank heaven. That's a miracle."

Mabel laughed. "Thank the new tenant. Apparently their damage deposit paid for repairs."

"Have they arrived yet?"

"Nope, but boxes keep arriving. Susanne says there are a dozen stacked by the door to #402. And there's a mystery."

"Another one?"

Mabel laughed and opened the door, waving Henry through, "No one knows how the boxes get into the building. No one has seen a delivery driver. No one has seen anyone taking things up to the fourth floor. Susanne is freaking out." She lowered her voice as she pushed the elevator button. The door opened. As it shut she said, "Nic offered to let her stay at his place."

"No!" Henry gasped.

"I know!" said Mabel, "I can't imagine the building without Susanne." She stepped out on the second floor. "Glad you're back," she said as the door shut.

Henry tried not to hyper-ventilate. Susanne had to stay. She had to.

MORE BOXES
#11

Originally scheduled: June 14, 2024

Shirley sat in the audience of Theatre on the Edge. While she listened to the chatter before the performance, she pondered boxes.

Specifically, she pondered boxes labelled "Occupant #402-325 Alex Street." They were all the same size: square boxes about two feet wide, high, and deep. They made a uniform stack against the wall on the fourth floor. Some seemed to give off an energy.

Shirley had snuck up to the fourth floor to marvel as the stack grew to the ceiling and stretched along the wall.

Most older ladies were skilled at being unnoticed; Shirley prided herself in being a master of invisibility, but whoever was dropping these boxes off was next level. Even she, who knew every trick and every secret hiding corner in the building, had yet to see a box bearing intruder.

Boxes appeared throughout the day and night. No door openings or foot falls marked their arrival. They'd been found in the entrance hall and each floor. There was no consistency.

It was a mystery, and Shirley didn't like it. She wanted to be the only mystery at 325 Alex Street. Not including the mystery of #402, of course. That wasn't so much a mystery as a tragedy.

Behind her, Mayor Harrison asked Counselor Cannon about preparations for the upcoming 55+ Games, and whether Bryan Kassa had enough volunteers.

Shirley pondered what sport she could compete in. She wasn't spry enough for pickle ball or dragon boat racing, but perhaps she was accurate enough pitching horseshoes? Horseshoe Club president Ben had told her she had a good arm the time she'd tried it.

A few rows ahead of her, Susanne and Nic sat together, each staring blankly at the stage. Trouble there.

Counselor Cannon asked the mayor something about media coverage at various venues, and suddenly Shirley had an idea.

A trip to the spy store in Kelowna was in order.

The lights dimmed, and she turned her mind to the performance.

DO WE HAVE RATS?
#12

Originally scheduled: June 21, 2024

It was after midnight. Dimity and Mabel had been sitting on the ratty couch practicing. Dimity had been playing guitar for a while, but her determination to spend the summer taking music lessons until their classes at Okanagan College started up again, had led Mabel to learn bass. Chris joined in on fiddle or penny whistle when they had a song recognizable enough.

Dimity and Mabel enjoyed playing together each evening, but they did not appreciate the pointed looks and yawns from Marcus, just because he slept on the couch. They couldn't practice in the bedroom, because Chris was already sleeping in there.

"That's enough," Marcus growled at the girls. "You should stop now. Go to bed."

"That's rude," said Mabel. "You should deal with those anger issues."

"Yeah," said Dimity, "maybe go to Mike's Meditation classes."

"I just want to go to sleep," he sighed. "Please get off my bed."

"Did you hear that?" said Dimity glancing to the ceiling as she put her guitar in its case.

"I just hear bass thumping in my ears," said Marcus.

Mabel glared at him, but tilted her head, concentrating.

"There!" said Dimity. "Did you hear that thud?"

Marcus shrugged. "Just rats jumping around."

"Ew! Don't be gross. We don't have rats!"

He laughed.

Mabel looked at Dimity in alarm, "We don't, do we?"

Dimity rolled her eyes.

"Maybe it's the box dude!" squawked Mabel. She would have leapt from the couch, but it was saggy and tended to grab butts. Dimity gave her a push that lifted Mabel and propelled her to the door.

"Look!" she said. "It's another box for #402!"

"Of course, it is," yawned Marcus. "Could you please let me go to bed now?"

When the girls went into the bathroom, Marcus looked into the hall. He spotted a tawny tail disappearing through the hole in the corner ceiling tile. Not a rat, after all.

DARN INTERLOPER!
#13

Originally scheduled: July 5, 2024

Henry sat at his window with his leg propped up and watched the world outside. Below, a green VW covered with butterflies and flowers drove by. "Hello, Sheila the Bug," he said to the empty room, remembering how the car's owner, his English teacher, seeing both his crush and his paralyzing shyness, had put him in Susanne's novel study group. Even at SAS, Susanne had been amazing.

He was still a fool for Susanne. He'd rented this apartment after Susanne was interviewed on the news about the incidents in #402. He'd been so happy that she'd been brave enough to stay here, and happier still that a suite became available in her building.

For five years he'd been taking his time, cultivating her affections, growing their friendship as they passed one another in the halls. After five years, he was finally ready to make his move.

He hadn't counted on Nic from the café butting in. No one should be that handsome and that buff. How could a gaming nerd compete? Even though Susanne regularly went with Henry for gaming nights and bubble tea, that hadn't fueled any passion yet.

A knock on the door broke his revery. He hitched his

crutches under his arms and hobbled to the door. Outside, he found a brown bag on one of the ubiquitous boxes for #402. Mouth watering aromas wafted from the bag. He called, "Thank you!" to the empty hallway.

Inside its to-go container, the food was still warm. There was rice, some type of meat, mixed vegetables and a sauce. It was spicy and flavourful. He groaned as his taste buds danced their appreciation.

He hoped the gifter was Susanne, but thought it was more likely from the dela Cruzes next door. He knew Susanne's culinary skills weren't this good. Still, it didn't matter she couldn't cook gourmet meals. He loved her for other things. Her smile. Her laugh. That twinkle in her eye when she thought something was funny. The way she was nice to everyone.

A girl as great as Susanne didn't come along every day.

He needed to do something dramatic to finally win her heart. But what?

IT'S THE BOXES
#14

Originally scheduled: July 12, 2024

Sofia dela Cruz felt the least they could do for their poor neighbour was send him over the occasional meal. Her husband Angelo grumbled that he didn't work hard to feed the neighbourhood, but he worked at a restaurant and brought home enough left-overs to share. Between listening to baby Maggie's screaming next door, his unrequited crushing on Susanne, and falling down the stairs, things had been rough for poor Henry lately.

Maggie's screaming hadn't abated in four months. The parenting websites said that when the teeth were all through, the baby would be quiet. They lied. Sofia talked to the doctor. He said it was colic that could take a year or so to disappear, but not to worry, she would get over it eventually.

This was not a comfort.

At this rate, Maggie would be an only child, because they couldn't handle another year of no sleep.

Sofia was sure it'd gotten worse since the boxes started stacking up.

It was astonishing how whenever she bundled Maggie up and walked the SABNES Trail, she was quiet and content. When they went visiting friends or were at the restaurant Angelo's parents owned, she never made a peep.

Even Angelo noticed the difference. Over Maggie's howls one night he said, "Maybe it's time to buy a house." He put his hands over his ears. "I could call Tall Tom and we can get him looking for something. What do you think?"

"A house?" Sofia gasped. "A real house? With a yard?"

Angelo nodded. "It'll have to be something small. Maybe in Canoe. I don't know. We'll see what Tall Tom can find."

Maggie had stopped crying and looked between her parents.

"It's the boxes, isn't it?" said Sofia.

Angelo didn't meet her eyes. "I'm not superstitious," he finally said, bouncing baby Maggie up and down. "But I want to get away from those boxes."

Maggie stopped crying, looked him right in the eyes, and gave him the first genuine smile she'd ever made, and then she reached up to pat his cheek.

WE HEAR NOISES
#15

Originally scheduled: July 19, 2024

Residents of 325 Alex were walking to the Rotary Marine Peace Park to see Dimity and Mabel play together with some other music school students at Wednesday on the Wharf.

"I miss the old route straight up Lakeshore to the crossing," said Henry. "The elevation of this underpass is hard to do on crutches."

Susanne laughed. "It must be almost time to start walking without them?"

Chris, who was carrying a small fiddle case on their back and a penny whistle in their pocket, said, "It could be worse. We could be hauling a double bass."

"Where's Marcus tonight?" asked Susanne.

"He said his welding class has a farewell party," shrugged Chris. "He didn't want to come."

Mabel scowled. "He told me he's heard all our songs nine hundred and sixty-seven times and that he was sure we'd be great and to 'make like Henry and break a leg.'"

"Well, I'm excited to hear you play," interjected Sofia dela Cruz, shifting baby Maggie who was burbling and kicking happily. "Don't you think, Angelo?"

Angelo would have preferred to be with Marcus, but nodded. Angelo's believed *Happy wife: happy life.*

They were among the first to arrive at the park. They spread blankets and settled in front of the bandstand while Dimity and Mabel joined a group from the music school.

After they'd warmed up, a good crowd had gathered.

"Next stop, Roots and Blues," said Henry.

"Everyone begins somewhere," said Susanne. "They may have great things ahead! Hush. They're starting."

The crowds were good and the music was fun. Henry hopped with Susanne in a semblance of dancing. Dela Cruzes swayed and bounced.

When Mabel and Dimity joined them after the performances, no one mentioned any mistakes they'd noticed.

As they walked home, Dimity said, "It's too bad the tenant in #202 didn't come. I put an invitation under their door."

Mabel spun and walked backwards, "Are we sure #202 is even alive?"

"They are," said Angelo. "We hear noises from below. You know, footsteps, talking, doors shutting. It must be from below, as #402 is empty, right?"

The group grew quiet. Wondering.

"Sometimes, I leave #202 food, and it's always gone," added Sofia. "The plates are returned at my door with a thank you note."

"I love your cooking," said Henry. "It's so kind of you to share. I appreciate it."

Sofia grinned.

"Look," gasped Henry, waving his crutch. "There's a light on in #402."

I HEAR NOTHING!
#16

Originally scheduled: August 2, 2024

Susanne was afraid of being stuck in a moving box, so she ignored the elevator. The rest of the residents of 325 Alex who'd been at Wednesday on the Wharf followed along behind her.

"I'm taking the elevator," said Henry. "I'll meet you all at the top!" He held the 'door open' button until he heard everyone on the third floor. He didn't want to risk being on the fourth floor alone.

"Excuse me," he said to Mabel, who was blocking his exit when he got to the fourth floor. There wasn't room in the small hallway for the three students, the delaCruz family, Susanne and him, but there was more room then there'd been that morning, because all the boxes had disappeared.

"Where are they?" whispered Dimity.

"Inside, obviously," said Chris.

Angelo rested his ear against the door to #402. He put his finger to his lips and everyone immediately hushed.

"What do you hear?" whispered Sofia.

"Nothing," Angelo whispered back.

"Back away!" hissed Susanne, "What if they open the door?"

Angelo rolled his eyes, but he stepped back.

Henry turned to Susanne. "We should go into in your suite."

She unlocked her door and they all filed inside before she thought to ask why they should come in.

"Wow!" said Dimity, looking around. "I love your skylight! It's so much brighter in here than in our apartment."

"Thanks," said Susanne as she dropped into the couch and Artemis leapt into her lap. "I don't think there's a mystery here. The new tenant has just arrived."

"We should welcome them," said Sofia. "Bring them something to eat."

"We have cheezies," offered Chris.

"Those are MY cheezies," said Mabel. "They're my reward for playing in public for the first time. You can give something from your cupboard."

"My cupboard is bare," muttered Chris.

"Never mind!" said Sofia. "I have something. I baked *pandesal* today. Should I get some now?"

"Maybe we should give them a chance to settle in?" said Henry. "They've only been in the building a couple of hours. Maybe they're tired from moving all those boxes?"

Right then, a long, cackling laugh straight out of a horror movie shook the walls and rattled the dishes in Susanne's cupboard.

Everyone stared at each other their eyes immense, as it went on and on, and then both baby Maggie and Artemis the cat started to screech.

HAUNTED?
#17

Originally scheduled: August 9, 2024

"I'm staying at your mother's," said Sofia over the wails of the baby. "I am not staying another night in this building!" She blinked away tears and wagged a finger at her husband. "Angelo, you call Tall Tom tonight! You tell him we need a house tomorrow!"

If she wanted to stay with his mother, things were serious. Angelo wrapped his arms around his wife. He squeeze her with one arm, while with the other he tried to rub Maggie's back in a soothing way so she'd stop screeching. "We'll go for a walk. Come on." He gave an apologetic shrug to the others in the room and followed Sofia out.

"Maybe we should *all* move," said Mabel. That laugh was the freakiest thing I've ever heard."

"I can't move," sighed Chris. "I can't afford to." They swallowed. "In fact, I can't afford to live here if you guys leave. Don't go."

"I won't go," assured Dimity. "I need to be close to the music school. Cory said he wants to hire me to teach beginner guitar in the fall. But Mabel's right. That laugh was freaky. Maybe someone should knock on the door and tell them to turn their TV down?"

"There's no way that was a TV," said Henry.

"Oh, please," said Dimity. "What else could it be?"

"I vote for 'Demon Spawn,'" said Mabel. "#402 is probably a Hellmouth."

Everyone stared at her.

She shrugged. "You know, like the high school in *Buffy*? It would make sense, wouldn't it?"

"Susanne," said Henry with a hushed voice. "Maybe you should tell them what happened five years ago."

Susanne shivered and buried her face in Artemis's fur. "I've been in counseling trying to forget what happened. I don't want to re-hash it now."

Dimity looked from Henry's weary face to Susanne's wary one. "Wait. What? I thought the whole '#402 is haunted' thing was a joke."

"Not joke," said Susanne.

"But, it's not haunted," said Henry.

"That's worse," said Chris.

"So the story's not just someone's vivid imagination?" asked Mabel.

"I wish," said Susanne.

WORSE
#18

Originally scheduled: August 16, 2024

Marcus's welding course was finished. His apprenticeship at Tolko started on Monday.

He was moving at last. He was looking forward to good sleep. No more struggling to fit on a too short couch. No more amateur musicians keeping him awake as they played the same song a thousand times. No more annoying commute. No more weird noises or giant cage giving him nightmares.

He'd rented a furnished room of his own in a mobile home park across the highway from the mill and he could not get there fast enough. He'd packed his bag and was leaving today. #402 was the last straw.

When the landlord of 325 Alex had texted Marcus, asking if he could do some metalwork to get apartment #402 ready for the new tenant, Marcus had readily agreed. Fixing a grill, a railing or piece of furniture wouldn't be a big challenge, and he needed the money. It was weird that he had to sign a Non-Disclosure Agreement about what he saw there.

He hadn't thought at that there could be anything really wrong up there.

Sure, he'd heard the hushed tones whenever any of the residents mentioned that suite, but Marcus lived in a rational world. He didn't believe in supernatural nonsense.

He knew Susanne said it should never be rented, that it was unethical.

He'd thought they were all exaggerating. He thought it was all just a joke on the newest guy in the building.

It wasn't.

It was worse than he could have imagined.

The -02 apartments ran the length of the building, with the living room window facing Alex Street and the bedroom window facing the city's Inner Core parking lot. All the windows on the parking lot side had bars. They were very artistic bars, but they were still bars. Apartment #402 didn't just have bars on the bedroom window, though. It had bars around the entire bedroom, including the ceiling and the floor. The cage door had a padlock the size of a dinner plate. His job was to cut out and remove all the bars.

Who—or what—needed a cage eight feet square?

But the cage wasn't the worst part.

There were dark stain everywheres. It was spattered on the walls and on the ceiling. It was in streaks across the floor. The stain was darkest next to the door, as if someone—or something—had been trying to escape and hadn't made it.

CAT'S EYE VIEW
#19

Originally scheduled: August 23, 2024

Shirley John was fast asleep in her recliner when she was jolted awake by maniacal laughter.

She grabbed the TV remote and kept hitting the mute button, but the cackle continued. It was a minute before she realized her TV wasn't on. The laughter reverberated through the building.

"Not again!" she muttered.

She flipped the lever to lift the recliner and tilt her out.

It had been years since creepy noises had caused troubles at 325 Alex. Five years, in fact.

If you didn't include the noise Shirley herself made in her secretive excursions through the building, there hadn't been any alarming noises since the last tenant of #402 had been taken out of the building on a stretcher.

"Cougar!" she called. "Psst, psst, psst!" She looked around the apartment, but the little tawny cat was nowhere. She grabbed the cat treats and opened the door to the hall cautiously, in case any of the students were investigating the awful noise, but their door was tightly shut.

"Cougar!" she hissed and rattled the treats.

An enquiring meow made Shirley look up to the corner of the ceiling where a hole in the acoustic tile was filled with a feline face. Shirley shook the treats again and Cougar leapt to the floor and sauntered into the apartment.

As Cougar ate, Shirley detached the miniature camera mounted on Cougar's collar and connected it to her computer.

The little cat strolled down to the bedroom while Shirley scanned the video of the cat's eye view of the hidden world within the walls and between the floors of 325 Alex Street.

"There you are!" She stopped the video and enlarged the image. She advanced the video slowly, working out how it'd been done. Very clever. Then she scanned ahead until it happened again, and ahead again. She smiled to herself.

WHAT WOMAN?
#20

Originally scheduled: September 6, 2024

Susanne was standing on the sidewalk about to go into the café for a quiche when through the window she saw Nic engrossed in conversation with the most beautiful woman she'd ever seen. She looked like she could be international super-model with her height, super-stylish clothes, makeup, and hair. What was she doing in Salmon Arm?

The woman cupped Nic's bicep, speaking earnestly, then she leaned over and kissed him.

Susanne's heart leapt into her throat.

She prided herself on being rational, on thinking the best of people, on not leaping to conclusions, but Susanne was leaping big time, and when she landed she knew this: Nic was a two-timing jerk!

The woman threw her head back, shaking long tousled hair like she was in a shampoo ad. She gave Nic a beaming smile, twiddled her fingers in a wave and turned to leave.

Susanne stepped away from the door as the woman pushed through.

"Excuse me," said Susanne, stepping out of her way.

The woman looked her up and down, raised one perfectly groomed brow, and sauntered down the street.

"Well," said Susanne as she watched the sashaying hips and statuesque posture that seemed to be attracting every eye on the street, "she's definitely not from around here."

She went into the café and got into line for her quiche.

Nic was back behind the counter. Aside from a slightly heightened complexion and a bead of perspiration around his hair-line, he was his normal, gorgeous self. "Hey, Susanne," he grinned when she got to the front of the line. "Quiche and coffee, two creams, one sugar?"

She wasn't sure whether she was happy he knew her order so well or if she was mortified that she was so predictable. She looked up at the menu board, ready to prove him wrong and then sighed. "Yes, please." She scanned her card. She really wanted quiche today.

Facing away as he poured her coffee, Nic said, "Oh, Susanne. I know we had talked about going to that concert at Song Sparrow Hall tonight, but I need to cancel. Sorry."

"Ah," said Susanne, accepting her coffee. "Hey, who was the glamorous woman who just left?"

Colour rose in Nic's face as he stammered, "Woman? What woman?"

"Oh, Nic," she said. "It seems we've reached the end of a beautiful friendship."

From further down the line of customers, she heard an emphatic, "YES!"

VISITORS
#21

Originally scheduled: September 13, 2024

From the top perch on her cat tree, Artemis the tuxedo cat looked out the fourth floor window and studied the street below. It seemed to her that there were far more grey headed humans than usual strolling along Alex Street. They seemed clustered in small, laughing groups in matching jackets, looking in store windows, and filling café patios with animated chatter, oblivious to the drama unfolding at 325 Alex.

On the middle perch of the cat tree curled tiny Cougar, who'd arrived inside the apartment a couple of hours ago with her rodent breath and entitled air. Artemis didn't know how Cougar got into the suite, and didn't really care. They'd had a good race around, dumping books and plates, and it'd been great fun. Now Cougar was asleep and Artemis was watching the street.

She saw Lorne and his dog Lexi with their stack of papers. Not far behind Lorne walked the lady from #202, Cougar's human. She camouflaged among all the other grey-haired people, so Lorne didn't notice her. He was handing people copies of his paper and grinning broadly. Lexi looked back suspiciously, but Lexi didn't talk.

Next door, in #402 there were interesting noises: thumping, scraping, and the hums and buzzes of various machines at work. Cougar would know what was happening, Cougar saw everything and recorded it all with the button-sized camera mounted on her collar.

Artemis wondered where Susanne was. She'd spent the night alternately weeping on her bed or muttering curses and stomping back and forth.

Henry from the third floor had knocked on the door four times.

The first time he'd asked her to join him for dinner. Susanne had called through the door, "Go away, Henry."

The second time he'd offered to take her to a concert where she could "show that jerk he didn't mean a thing." Susanne had thanked him for the thought, but asked him to please leave.

The third time, he said he knew a guy who would ensure Nic never broke anyone's heart again. Susanne had laughed, told him no, it was fine. Henry should just go.

The fourth time, he said he had take-out with him. Would she just open the door and take it? She needed to eat. The aromas coming through the door made Artemis's mouth water.

Susanne opened the door and invited Henry in.

Now Susanne was gone and the noises coming from #402 were louder.

Artemis looked for Cougar, but she'd vanished.

SCARRED FOR LIFE #22

Originally scheduled: September 20, 2024

Chris texted Marcus to ask how his apprenticeship was going and to probe as gently as possible into what had happened to scare him away. Chris knew it had something to do with #402. If Marcus knew the secret, Chris wanted to know, too.

"You don't want to know," texted Marcus. "Trust me on this."

Regardless, he'd agreed to meet Chris half-way. They decided to watch the final double-feature of the season at the drive-in in Enderby. Chris got a ride from a friend, and Marcus drove his new car, purchased with his first apprentice wages. It was an old rust bucket, but it was better than walking or riding his folding bike on the highway.

As they drove through Enderby, Chris thought it felt pleasantly peaceful, as if a lot of concentrated positivity had settled there. "Nice," he thought. "I wonder what caused that?"

Chris met up with Marcus at the concession. They stocked up on popcorn, nachos, and candy and made their way back to Marcus's car.

"Well?" asked Chris as they settled into the passenger seat. "What was so horrible that it made you leave that unceremoniously?"

Marcus wanted to mention the uncomfortable couch and obnoxious musicians, but held his tongue. Chris had been kind to offer him place to crash while he did his course, even if it hadn't been comfortable.

"Look," said Marcus. "I don't want to scar you for life. I still get nightmares about what I saw in #402."

"I can take it," said Chris.

"Okay," said Marcus. "Don't say I didn't warn you." Outside the car, the opening credits of the movie started on the big screen.

Marcus told Chris about what he'd seen in #402: The cage. The dark stains. He shuddered.

Chris sat with his mouth agape looking from the movie to Marcus. "No way."

"Yes, way."

"What was the stain?"

Marcus stared ahead as the characters on the screen entered the haunted house. "Pretty obvious what it had to be, don't you think?"

Ahead of them, the screen turned red.

LAUGHTER
#23

Originally scheduled: October 4, 2024

Henry was about to knock on Susanne's door, when the elevator opened behind him..

"Hey," said Chris with a furtive look down the hall. "How's it going?"

"It's going fine," said Henry. "What are you doing up here?"

There was a rattle that shook the building and made Chris yelp.

"It's just the train," said Henry, but then that horrible laughter started again.

Chris put his hands over his ears. "I learned something"

Henry nodded and knocked firmly on #401. "We should tell Susanne."

When she opened the door, Henry pushed Chris through. "We need to hear what he knows about #402." In the hall, the noise was unbearable.

"Is it about that laughing?" said Susanne with an unnaturally loud voice as she squinted slightly at them. Fluorescent orange earplugs protruded through her hair.

Susanne shut the door behind them as Chris and Henry flopped onto the couch, leaving Susanne to pull up a kitchen chair. "Okay. What?"

Chris told them what Marcus had said about the cage and the stains. "Does that fit with your memories of what happened five years ago, Susanne?"

She shrugged. "Maybe?"

"I think we need to get in there and have a look for ourselves," said Henry. "You game, Chris?"

Chris shuddered. "No way. That's break and enter. I'm not having any of that."

Henry looked over to Susanne. "How about you?"

She shook her head. "I don't think we have to resort to illegal actions."

Henry threw his arms in the air and gave an exasperated sigh. "Come on!"

"No, really," said Susanne. "I think we just need to look in the right place."

"You've been in the building longest," said Chris. "Don't you know the most?"

"The night the ambulance came, my parents saw it on the news. I was only nineteen, and they wanted to protect me. They hustled me home to them in Kelowna and kept the news off. I didn't want to know the details, so I didn't look. When I came back a few weeks later, it was old news. No one talked about it. There were only ridiculous rumours. But the police had to have investigated. We just need to read those reports."

"Huh," said Henry. "That's actually a good idea."

"Yes," said Susanne, rolling her eyes. "I get quite a lot of them."

NOBODY TALKED
#24

Originally scheduled: October 11, 2024

"His name was Mr. Moreno. Juan Moreno," Susanne said, wishing she had a more comfortable chair. "He had already been here a few years when I moved in. He was quiet and kept to himself, but he always said hello when we met in the halls. He didn't deserve what happened to him. No one deserves to be shredded like that."

"Shredded?" said Chris. "What do you mean by that?"

There was a knock at the door. Henry went to answer it and returned with Dimity and Mabel.

"We want to know, too."

Chris scowled at them, "It's probably better if you don't."

"We live here, too," said Mabel. "We deserve the truth."

"Folks don't always get what they deserve," said Henry. "Susanne was just telling us that."

Susanne rolled her eyes. "Let them hear. Knowledge is power."

"Unless it gives you nightmares," muttered Chris. "You don't have to live with these two."

"Oh hush," said Dimity. "Go on, Susanne."

"Mr. Moreno was nice enough, but there was

something weird about his apartment. When he'd been in or out, an awful smell hovered on the landing."

"Awful like skunky?"

"Not pot. Pungent. Like the world's worst litter box or something. It was just really gross."

"Hmm," said Henry, glancing to the corner near the bathroom where Artemis's covered litter box was camouflaged under a table.

"And there were stange noises," said Susanne. "Loud. Kinda like a motorcycle revving, but higher pitched. Sometimes rumbly, almost like thunder."

"And then one day, I came home from work at the hospital, and I found Mr. Moreno lying in the hallway, bleeding. His door was shut, but those noises were loud. And something was thudding against the door."

"I called the ambulance and stayed with him until they came.

"They took him away, but the police came to ask me what happened, because his injuries were so strange, they went inside his apartment, but I wasn't home then. Then the press came. When my parents saw me on the news, they took me back to Kelowna. By the time I came back, no one said anything. I never saw Mr. Moreno again."

"And nobody talked about it?" asked Mabel, incredulously. "This is Salmon Arm! News flies around here!"

"When I came back the news was all about fire evacuations," shrugged Susanne.

"And wildlife sightings," added Henry, "because of the fires. There were deer, bear, and even cougars sighted everywhere that year."

YET MORE BOXES
(Bonus episode)

From her perch behind the ceiling vent, Cougar watched the occupant of #402.

Boxes lined the walls and more of them were open in piles of tantalizing invitation.

Cougar waited for the right moment to sneak through then vent to explore this paradise of boxes. She was stealthy. She could do it undetected. No one in 325 Alex ever saw her, unless she wanted to be seen.

The person grunted and hoisted a machine, kicking its empty box out of the way as they carried the heavy item into the bedroom.

Cougar quivered with longing. This was the time! Cougar jumped. She leapt into one box and then into another. This was cat heaven! One box had towels, such soft, fluffy, cozy towels! Cougar sighed and curled into a ball. Her body relaxed and she drifted in bliss.

Well, hello little one," said an amused voice. "Where did you come from?"

Cougar yawned to hide her panic and considered her options. She blinked lazily as she identified her route.

The person reached toward her, but Cougar was gone, through the boxes and away, vowing she'd never again fall for the temptation of boxes.

DESIST!
#25

Originally scheduled: October 18, 2024

Dimity and Mabel had been working on the first eight bars of their duet for a solid hour and were finally making progress. Mabel's bass was finally consistently on the beat, and mostly of decent rhythm. Dimity's guitar chord progressions were much smoother.

They were interupted by a hammering on the door. When Mabel answered it, a super-model was standing in the hall.

"That is enough!" she drawled, with emphatic pause between each word she spoke. "I can not take another moment of this! We can hear you down the street! I want to eat my sushi in peace! I insist you desist!"

"Excuse me?" blinked Mabel, so stunned by the beauty in front of her that her hearing hadn't worked. "Resist what?"

"DESIST!" shouted the woman. "NOW!" She spun on her heel and stomped down the stairs.

"Who was that?" asked Dimity when Mabel returned to her seat. She had a dazed look.

"I have no idea, but I think I get why Susanne and Nic broke up."

"Oh," said Dimity. "Her. How did she manage to get into the building?"

Mabel shrugged and started to put her bass in its case. "I guess we should stop playing for now."

"We were finally getting that tricky bit."

"Yeah, but we can't annoy the passers-by."

"You know," said Dimity, "I don't believe she came in from the street. The insulation is better than that. We get hardly any street noise inside, so how could our noise get outside?"

"If she didn't come from the street, where did she come from?"

Dimity just looked at her.

"Oh! Is she the elusive tenant in #202?"

"Does she look like the kind of person who doesn't want to be noticed? I don't think she's from #202. I think she's from #402."

"Excellent point. Either way it means we have a neighbour who hates our music. That's not good."

THROUGH THE SKYLIGHT
#26

Originally scheduled: November 1, 2024

Henry, Chris, Dimity, and Mabel were sitting in Susanne's apartment as Dimity and Mabel told the others about their suspicions about the identity of the tenant in #402.

There was a noise overhead and they looked up to see a crow looking in at them through the skylight.

"Susanne, if you have a skylight, does that mean #402 has a skylight?" asked Henry.

"I suppose so."

"Oh!" sighed Chris. "We could look into the suite through the skylight if we had a way to get onto the roof."

"We have," Susanne nodded. "There's an access stair behind the elevator. I have a key."

They all turned to stare at her.

Susanne blushed. "Well, yeah. Part of my lease includes roof garden access."

"Roof garden?!" Four voices chimed in unison.

Dimity blinked, "There's a roof garden?"

Susanne shrugged, "There's not any more. Back when Mr. Moreno was around, he kept it nice. He had a private spot with potted trees over on his side. I just had a gravity lounger and pot of petunias on my side. It was nice to sit up there and read on a summer's evening. But after he was carried off in the ambulance, access was blocked, and I knew that all the plants would just be dead and my lounger would be rags, so it was too depressing to go back."

"What are we waiting for?" said Chris. "Let's look through the skylight and see what's there!"

Susanne muttered, "Invasion of privacy," but she took a key off a nail inside a kitchen cupboard and handed it to Henry.

The lock was sticky and took some wiggling, but eventually the key turned and they all trooped up the narrow stairs. They needed to unlock another door, and then they were on the roof.

"What a great view!" said Dimity admiring the lake over the railway tracks. "I can't believe you stopped coming up here!"

Henry looked through Susanne's skylight into the room they'd just vacated. "It's hard to see. There must be some UV coating on it or something."

"There's the skylight for #402," said Chris waving their arm toward a row of wooden boxes filled with dead branches. "This would have been a nice veranda when it was maintained."

Henry examined the skylight. "This one is newer than Susanne's." He leaned over. "Huh."

"What?" Chris pushed him over to get a view. "Wow. Is that legal?"

Susanne, Dimity and Mabel squeezed in straining to make out the very unconventional living room below them.

"It looks like a news room," said Mabel.

WHAT ENEMY?
#27

Originally scheduled: November 8, 2024

Chris, Dimity, Mabel, Susanne, and Henry stepped back from the skylight on the roof of 325 Alex and looked at one another with baffled expressions.

"Why would someone have a news studio in their living room?" Dimity sat on the edge of a planter. "That's just weird."

"Maybe the new tenant is a secret agent, broadcasting secret reports to the enemy," suggested Chris.

"What enemy?" said Henry.

"Secret reports from Salmon Arm?" laughed Susanne.

"You never know," said Chris. "A lot of really interesting people live in Salmon Arm. I heard there's a guy who was with the RCMP Security Service. Why would he be here and not spies?"

Susanne rolled her eyes. "There has to be a more logical explanation."

"Do you think that satellite dish over there has something to do with it?" said Mabel.

"Susanne went over and studied the metre wide parabollic dish. "This wasn't here before."

"That's bigger than a standard household dish," said Chris.

Dimity gave a shiver. "This whole thing makes me

nervous."

"Henry?"

"What? Why are you looking at me?"

Susanne put her hands on her hips. "Is this your satellite dish for watching those nerdy movies?"

"Hey! That's not very nice." Then he blushed and added, "I just have a small satellite receiver in my window."

"What do you think that is?" asked Mabel, pointing to sparkling shards around the side of the skylight frame.

Chris bent down, "Looks like bits of glass. I guess the previous skylight broke."

"Why is there glass on the roof then? Shouldn't it fall inward?" asked Mabel.

"Not if whatever broke it was bursting out from the inside," said Henry.

Susanne picked a clump of tawny fur off one of the dried cedar branches. "You don't think…"

Henry stared at the tuft of fur, then down at the skylight and broken glass. "No way."

BEHIND DOOR #402
(Bonus episode)

The police were initially baffled by the alarming wounds they noted on Juan Moreno. The EMTs took the man away, sirens blaring down Lakeshore. The constables stood on the landing pondering the closed door of his apartment.

"Man or beast?" said the older one, "What's your guess?"

"Only someone with knives on their knuckles could slash like that," replied his young partner.

The older officer put an ear against the door. "I don't hear anything, but something tells me I don't want to go in there."

"What do you think, conservation officer or city animal control?"

"We can't wait. We have to see if anyone else is injured in there," said the older, somewhat apologetically. He jumped back when there was a strange clanking noise from inside #402. There was a blood-curdling scream.

Both officers drew their weapons and reached for the doorknob, but before they could turn it, came a crash of exploding glass. There was pounding above their heads and something very large and tan flashed by the corridor window.

They ran to the window and watched a long tawny tail disappear behind blue bins.

"Conservation officer, it is," gasped the younger officer, reaching for his radio.

COUGAR THOUGHTS
#28

Originally scheduled: November 15, 2024

The city was quiet the night he escaped the cage, except for the siren. Occasional semi-trucks or cars passed on the highway, but they were not his concern. He stalked the edges of the small lake, following the scent of the prey that had escaped him, the prey that he could scent wafting from that loud, wailing white vehicle.

He had not wanted the cold carcasses that had been left in colder steel bowls, but he had eaten them to defeat the hunger. He was not made for a cage. He had been a cub when he'd been brought to that cage. The human held him tightly and fed him from bottles. The human taught him to jump through hoops and sit on boxes.

The human gave him cold meat, that sometimes crunched with ice crystals.

He'd known there was more than the small space. He had scented the richness outside the windows.

He had longed for forests of unending green.

He had wanted trees to climb high high high until he pierced the blue sky beyond the glass above his head

He desired hot flesh, pulsing with life. He wanted the satisfaction of the hunt. He wanted to run, to spring, to tear, to devour.

The man who had caged him had forgotten that he

was no longer a cub, but a wild cat, grown. He outweighed the man now.

He had teeth and claws.

The man had no weapons except his wits, and a man who thinks he can keep a cougar as a pet has very few wits, indeed.

When the man, his prey, had escaped beyond his fortified door, there had been one way out.

The cougar had leapt through the skylight and gone searching for his prey.

He would not enter the building with its scents of blood and pungent anticeptic. But there were small beasts along the water. They would do for now.

WARNING:
Cougar sightings at McGuire Lake and SABNES Trail.
Trails closed until further notice.

ALL THERE IS TO KNOW
#29

Originally scheduled: November 22, 2024

Like her owner, Shirley John of #202, Cougar, the little tawny cat, liked to hide in the secret places of 325 Alex to see while unseen.

Unlike Shirley, who'd grown portly and somewhat slow moving, Cougar was lithe and agile. She could leap from floor to ceiling in a bound. She could open cupboard doors. She could fit into the smallest of openings. Through the button camera on her collar, Cougar was Shirley's eyes to secret places.

Thanks to Cougar, Shirley knew all there was to know about what happened at 325 Alex. She knew about the little stash the students in #201 kept at the back of the bedroom closet. She knew about the satellite dish and pirated video games Henry Block had in #301. She knew about the cigars Angelo dela Cruz in #302 hid from Sofia. She knew that Susanna in #401 had boxes of steamy romance novels under her bed. She knew all about the new resident of #402. And at long last, she had solved the mystery of the boxes.

Since the store-front at 325 Alex was vacant, the big delivery companies were leaving boxes at the café. To get them from the café to #402 required a middle man.

Nic from the café might be a great server, but he was

not a good delivery man. And doing two jobs as the same time meant shoddy work.

He had #402's spare key. He collected boxes left at the café, but he had to bring them up between customers at the café. There was rarely time to carry a box all the way to the top, so if he was constantly dropping the boxes however far he could carry them before his phone buzzed to tell him to get back to work.

And every once in a while, he had a bit more time to get in and tidy the stack.

He was a man who liked to make a good impression. A handsome young man. Too young for Shirley, of course, but Shirley had her eyes on a jovial newspaperman.

The new resident wasn't living in the building yet. They were still renovating.

A crew worked quietly without bothering anyone else, except for the occasional buzz or thump.

Things were changing at 325 Alex. Was it for good or evil? Shirley was still thinking about that.

WHO ARE YOU?
#30

Originally scheduled: December 6, 2024

Henry was walking along Alex Street when he saw the woman. He was sure that she was the one Susanne had been talking about. How many statuesque super-model type folks wandered through downtown Salmon Arm?

She crossed the street and went into the Wild Water Clothing store.

Henry sat on the green spiral stairs beside the store and waited.

Thirty minutes later, when she came out of the store carrying two bags, he rose from the step and stuck out his hand as if to shake hers, "Hello there, I'm Henry Block."

She looked at his outstretched hand, glanced down at her two bag laden hands, shook her head, and walked away without saying a word.

"Hrmpf," grunted Henry. "She's definitely not from around here." He followed at what he hoped was a discreet distance, but when she popped out of the bookstore scowling, he froze.

"Why are you following me?" she demanded.

"I'm just going…um…to the stationary store," he said, waving up the block.

"Look, Harry Brock, I'm not stupid. Just tell me what you want." Her glare made him feel about the size of a hydrant.

Henry swallowed. He'd imagined a sane conversation. He didn't know how to respond to a banshee in attack mode. Finally he blurted, "How do you know Nic?"

She smirked and flipped her hair. "Jealous?"

He tried again. "You seem to be new to the area. I've known Nic a while. I was just wondering…"

Her mouth was smiling, but her eyes were not.

Henry re-started, "So, I thought I'd introduce myself. I'm Henry. I live at 325 Alex."

She raised both eyebrows.

Henry swallowed again and squeaked, "Who are you?"

She flipped her hair again and her chest rose dramatically and she enunciated each word as if she were a queen addressing her peasantry, "I…am…Desdemona Moreno."

She waited, as if expecting he to recognize the name.

"Oh," he said, suddenly making the connection. "Any relation to Mr. Moreno who lived at #402"

"My uncle," said Desdemona. "I have inherited his apartment following his recent death."

"That's great. Awesome," gulped Henry. "I mean, my condolences. Welcome to the neighbourhood, Desdemona Moreno." He took a deep breath and added, "We'd really like to talk to you."

YOU KNOW WHAT THEY SAY
#31

Originally scheduled: December 13, 2024

Henry had had to beg Susanne to even consider sitting down with Nic, and once she'd agreed, Nic claimed he didn't want to be with Desdemona and Susanne in the same room.

Eventually, however, they all agreed to meet like grown-ups over a piece of pie.

They sat at a table for four in the corner, Desdemona and Nic on one side, Henry and Susanne on the other.

Chris, Mabel, and Dimity tagged along and sat at a neighbouring table with their own pie. It was exam time at Okanagan College. Mabel assured them pie was excellent brainfood.

Henry introduced Desdemona as the new resident of #402.

"So what you're saying," said Susanne incredulously, "is that Mr. Moreno was okay? Even with all that blood loss, he survived?"

Desdemona nodded, "You know what they say about head wounds bleeding horrendously. Uncle Juan got a few good gashes, but a hundred stitches later, he was as good as new."

Susanne shook her head. "For the last five years I thought he was dead when I found him, five years ago."

"Nope," said Desdemona, cutting a forkful of cherry pie smothered in coconut cream topping. "You probably saved him by calling for an ambulance." She raised the fork of pie in a toast. "On behalf of the Moreno family, we thank you."

"But what happened?" asked Dimity, who had a blueberry stained tongue.

"Uncle Juan came to recover with us in Vancouver, and then he decided to stay a little longer and then that became a littler longer. I think he planned to return eventually, but he was hit by a bus at Hasting and Main and that was the end of him." She crossed herself and added, "May he rest in peace."

"So if you inherited #402, does that mean you inherited the building?" asked Chris. "I thought we were all paying rent."

Desdemona shrugged, "I only know I own #402. I don't know anything about the rest of the building."

"I have to go back to work," said Nic. "Is everyone all right now?" He looked directly at Susanne.

Henry coughed.

Susanne sighed. "If you mean will I hire a hitman to take you down for breaking my heart, no. I do have other friends." She smiled at the others around the table. "But Desdemona, you have to tell us. What is with all the recording equipment in your apartment?"

Desdemona laughed, "I think this is when I have to apologize for testing the sound system with that creepy laugh track. That was poor manners."

The others looked relieved.

"Anyway," she continued, "I have a Youtube channel

with over a million followers. I provide beauty tips. Speaking of, did you know there's an amazing clean cosmetic entrepreneur here in Salmon Arm? Missy was even on Dragon's Den!"

STEALTH
(Bonus episode)

Desdemona was confused by the comments left on her most recent video posting about the award winning lipstick made in Salmon Arm.

Sure, "So cute!" or "Ahhhh!" weren't too weird, but the ones that said things like "That is the most adorable creature I've ever seen!" took her aback.

Creature? Pardon me?

Then there were the ones that were positively baffling, "Wow! That's agile!" "She should be in Cirque du Soleil!" "So tiny and fluffy!"

At first she presumed there'd been a glitch, and these comments were meant for someone else's vlog, but her views were exploding. FOUR MILLION views of this video in twenty-four hours! She'd never had a video go viral like that.

She watched over and over trying to see what the commenters had seen. Finally, about the twentieth view she saw it: in the background, half-way through the video, a tiny feline head emerged from the ceiling vent. The small cat leapt lithely to the window ledge, climbed the curtains and sat staring at the camera from its perch on the top of the rod.

Ah, she thought. *I should invest in catnip.*

ALL IS CALM
#32

Inside her candle-lit apartment, Shirley John sat in her recliner, wine glass in hand, listening to Christmas music and patting her little cat. Cougar's purring filled the room.

"Do you think they'll ever figure things out?" she asked the cat with a chuckle.

Upstairs, she knew, the other residents had gathered in #401. She could imagine their delight as they ate a wonderful meal and exchanged gifts.

They'd pushed an invitation under her door, but she had her own perfect celebration planned. She would maintain her pesonal mystery for them at least a little longer.

"We'll miss you," Susanne said to Sofia, handing her a glass of punch. Maggie stood unsteadily, gripping Angelo's knee and grinning up at them to show off her four new teeth.

Sofia smiled wistfully, "I'll bring you some *Pandesal* for your birthday."

"Maybe you don't have to move now we know that Desdemona isn't a ghost, and Maggie is happier?

Angelo laughed, "Maggie has seen the backyard. There's no turning back now. It's just over on Beatty, so we'll still be in the neighbourhood."

Chris stood awkwardly, one hand in their pocket, wrapped around a note that said their rent had been paid for the next four months. They were going to be able to finish the college term and afford to eat. It was a miracle.

Henry turned to Dimity and Mabel. "Did I hear something about you two having big news?"

The women grinned at one another, "A music agent approached us about a recording deal. Someone apparently sent him a recording of us playing at Wednesday on the Wharf. He's arranged for us to make an album in the spring!"

Susanne joined them for an awkward three way hug.

Desdemona said, "I'll have to have you on my Youtube channel. Maybe we can feature you getting a makeover before shooting your album cover photos."

Mabel and Dimity grinned, before pondering whether this presumption that they needed a makeover was a veiled insult.

"So," said Dimity looking from Henry to Susanne. "Do you two have any news you want to share?"

Susanne shrugged, "Not really. Same ol' boring life on the fourth floor. Oh, but there is one thing. "Desdemona, how long have you actually been living in #402 now?"

"It's been over a month."

Susanned looked at Henry. "I believe you owe me ten dollars."

Artemis leapt onto her cat tree. Below, Lorne and Lexi stopped in front of 325 Alex. Lorne pushed an intercom button. Snow fell gently in the glow of street lights. Salmon Arm was at peace.

ACKNOWLEDGEMENTS

Thanks to Lorne Reimer of the Salmon Arm *Friday A.M.* for embracing so enthusiastically the project that became *325 Alex*. I pitched the project at Sweet Leaf over quiche, coffee and a sweet treat on March 4th, with a 'pilot episode' that was published as episode 1 only eleven days later.

Thanks to my husband John, for just rolling his eyes when I procrastinated my taxes by writing all thirty-two episodes of *325 Alex* in eight days. (But see, honey? I got EVERYTHING done on time anyway!)

Thanks to Tyner Gillies for police procedure information.

Thanks to the Salmon Arm Association of Writers for all the wonderful things they do to bring so many wonderful authors, editors, and publishers to Word on the Lake Writers' Conference here in Salmon Arm each year.

Thanks to all the readers who've been so keen and encouraging as the story released episode by episode. I appreciate your kind words!

Shawn
2024-10-25

ABOUT THE AUTHOR

(Photo by Ava Franklin Photography)

Shawn L. Bird (BA, MEd) is an educator, author, and poet in the beautiful Shuswap region of BC. Since her first novel was published in 2010, she has published twenty-five shorts, novellas, novels, or poetry books. She has also been published in ten anthologies including *Writing Better Fiction: Craft Tips From Some of Canada's Best Writers and Editors*.

Her short stories have been short-listed for the SiWC Storyteller Award or the Okanagan Short Story contest multiple times.

Her first novel, *Grace Awakening Dreams and Power,* was nominated for the Whistler Independent Book Award and her novella *Murdering Mr. Edwards* was nominated in the Lou Allin Memorial Best Crime Novella category of the 2019 Arthur Ellis Crime Writing Awards.

She is infamous for her Fluevog footwear which led to collaborating with artist Nikolette Jones on the series *Nikki Knox and her Shoes that Rock*.

Shawn plays the harp and trains her precocious miniature poodle in agility, rally obedience, and tricks. She enjoys several creative hobbies. She has a brilliant husband and some pleasant progeny.

Please visit
LintusenPress.ca
to learn more about our upcoming releases
and to see submission calls
for our future publications.

Thank you for leaving a review
on your favourite site or retailer
if you enjoyed this book.

**Here are some
other Lintusen Press titles
you may enjoy:**

GHOSTLY
13 tales from behind the veil

This spooky anthology features 13 ghost stories from authors Finnian Burnett, L. N. Hunter, Theric Jepson, Rob Nisbet, Lee F. Patrick, Alix Kelinda, Kaitlyn Petry, Shawn L. Bird, Marie Powell, Halli Reid, Leslie Wibberley, Jarrod K Williams, and Jeanna Mason Stay

THE DRAGON PROBLEM
a collaborative novel

The village of Zos has a dragon problem.

Follow the townsfolk as they deal with an evil dentist, a decrepit dragon, a musical milkmaid, and political shenanigans.

10 authors brainstormed this novel at When Words Collide Writers' Conference in 2023 and worked together to craft this entertaining tale.

NEW SPACES:
an anthology of sci-fi short stories

Within your mind and across the universe, there are new spaces to explore!

From Lintusen Press comes this collection of ten science fiction short stories from authors Finnian Burnett, Andrew G. Cooper, J. Paul Cooper, BC Deeks, Nancy Kilpatrick, Philip Mann, Lee F. Patrick, Halli Reid, KT Wagner, and Jarrod K. Williams.

SMALL SHIFTS:
short stories of fantastical transformation

Not all shifters turn into magnificent beasts. Sure, there are those humans who transform into wolves and bears, but this book is about the smaller creatures. Learn about the trials and tribulations of folks who turn into raccoons, hamsters, mosquitoes, or bumblebees. 11 delightful tales of Small Shifts.

THE DRABBLE ADVENT CALENDAR

A drabble is a story of precisely one hundred words. Here are 25 family friendly winter themed drabbles; one perfectly complete tidbit of story to savour each day leading up to Christmas from authors Carol Parchewsky, Chris McMahen, Finnian Burnett, Lee F. Patrick, Shawn L. Bird, and Tim Reynolds.